W9-AWJ-288

READING

RECOVERY

Maybe a Monster

by

Martha Alexander

Dial Books for Young Readers

E. P. Dutton, Inc. / New York

for all young trappers—especially Barry, Britt, Christopher, and John

I think I'll make a trap.

Wonder what I'll catch?

Maybe a monster!

I'd better go build a cage.

It might be enormous.
I'd better make a *big* cage.

Maybe it will have two heads.
I'd better make a place for them.

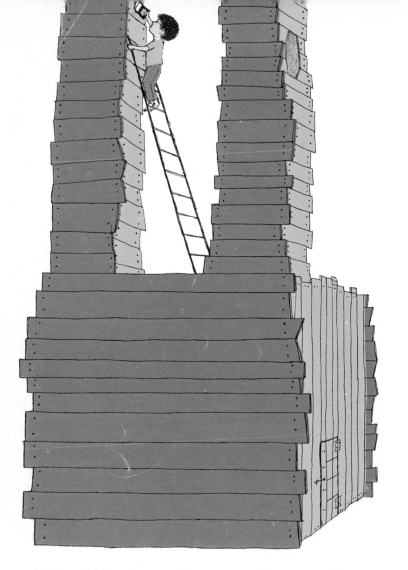

What if it shoots fire out of its nose?
I'd better cut holes for the fire to come out.

What if it has an enormous tail?
I'd better make tail space.

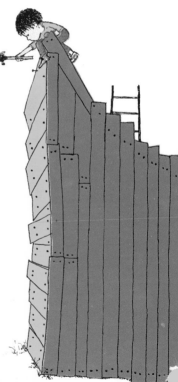

Maybe it will have big wings.
I'd better make wing space.

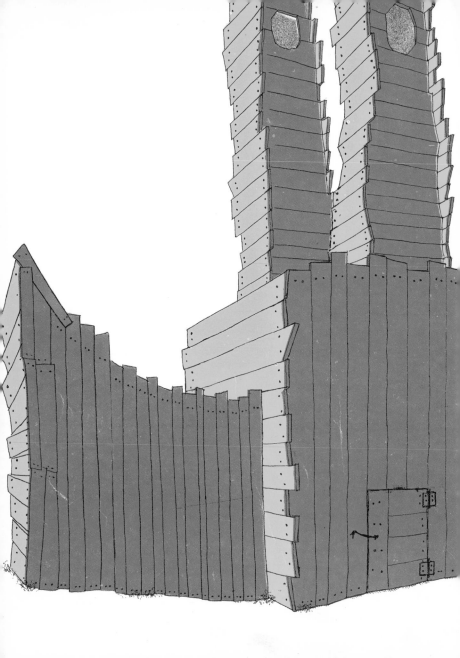

Now I'll go get the monster.

What if he's mean?

I'd better get protected.

I'll take my slingshot.

I'd better take my water pistol to put out the fire.

I'll wear my football stuff.

What if he won't come with me?
I'd better take some rope.

Now I'm ready.

Well, look what I caught!

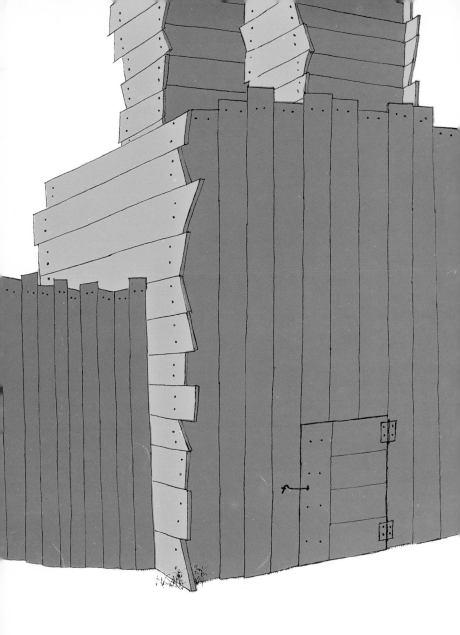

What's that?

It's a rabbit cage, stupid!

ABOUT THE AUTHOR

Martha Alexander was born in Augusta, Georgia, and lived in Hawaii for many years. She has worked in many fields of art including magazine illustration and teaching children's art classes, but now devotes her full time to writing and illustrating children's books. Among her many books are *I'll Protect You from the Jungle Beasts*, winner of the 1973 Christopher Award; *Nobody Asked* Me *if I Wanted a Baby Sister;* and her *Blackboard Bear* books.

Ms. Alexander now makes New York City her home.

DATE DUE			

E
ALE

Alexander, Martha G.

Maybe a monster.

8953